TYPHOON   ICKY

To Reena. Thanks for the SUPER idea,
and for all your encouragement and support! —S. B.

For the super Salibas —E. K.

STERLING CHILDREN'S BOOKS
New York

An Imprint of Sterling Publishing Co., Inc.
1166 Avenue of the Americas
New York, NY 10036

ISBN 978-1-4549-2703-7

Distributed in Canada by Sterling Publishing Co., Inc.
c/o Canadian Manda Group, 664 Annette Street
Toronto, Ontario M6S 2C8, Canada
Distributed in the United Kingdom by GMC Distribution Services
Castle Place, 166 High Street, Lewes, East Sussex BN7 1XU, England
Distributed in Australia by NewSouth Books
45 Beach Street, Coogee, NSW 2034, Australia

For information about custom editions, special sales, and premium and corporate purchases,
please contact Sterling Special Sales at 800-805-5489 or specialsales@sterlingpublishing.com.

Manufactured in China

Lot #:
2 4 6 8 10 9 7 5 3 1
07/18

sterlingpublishing.com

The artwork for this book was created digitally.

EVEN SUPERHEROES MAKE MISTAKES

By SHELLY BECKER · Illustrated by EDA KABAN

STERLING CHILDREN'S BOOKS

New York

When superheroes are not up to speed,
when they slip up, and trip up, and fail to succeed . . .

. . . they could cry, or deny, or claim it's not fair

or rip off their capes and quit in despair.

If they bake super-cakes with way too much salt,

they could shrug, "It was bakery bought—not *my* fault!"

If they bungle their speech at the Hero Convention, they could put on a light show, diverting attention.

If they space out and nab the wrong guys without thought,
they could choose to let bandits succeed with their plot!

But ashamed superheroes who goofed up somehow . . .

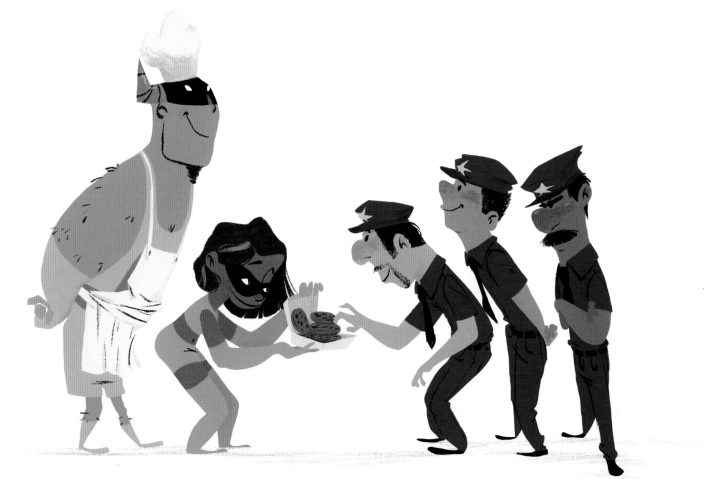

first STOP and consider what's best to do NOW.

If they wake late for boot camp the very first day,
they invent an alarm clock that works right away.

If last year they ruined the annual choir,
they train screechy voices and learn to sing higher.

If they didn't prepare any clean clothes to wear,

they still polish

their boots

and spiff up their hair.

But if superheroes can't take their errors in stride,
they might look for a way to excuse, blame, or hide.

If they bash through the planets while flying in space,

they could claim someone's cape was obstructing their face.

If they build a big bridge that doesn't sit right,
they could blame and call names—
a super-charged fight!

If their rescue attempt was NOT super-clever,
they could stock up supplies and hide out FOREVER.

When superheroes are not up to speed,

when they slip up, and trip up, and fail to succeed . . .

they *could* hang their heads down, they *could*, but they *don't!*
Because *real* superheroes just *wouldn't*, they *won't!*

Instead they remember perfection is rare,
And they choose super ways to respond when they err.

And using their powers as true heroes do . . .
they fix what they wrecked and apologize, too!

They fess up their mess-up. They learn from their blooper.
RESPONSIBILITY! THAT makes them SUPER!

It's okay if they blush.

It's okay if they quake.

It's okay if they super-regret their mistake!

But then they get up and get on with their day . . .

. . . saving the world in their most super way.